I Want to Be an Astronaut   by Byron Barton

HarperCollins_Publishers_

I Want to Be an Astronaut. Copyight © 1988 by Byron Barton. All rights reserved. Manufactured in China. For information address HarperCollins Children's Books, a division of HarperCollins Publishers, 195 Broadway, New York, NY 10007. Library of Congress Cataloging-in-Publicatiom Data: Barton, Byron. I want to be an astronaut. Summary: A young child wants to be an astronaut and goes on a mission into space. [1. Astronautics—Fiction] I. Title. PZ7.B2848Iwa 1988 [E] 87-24311 ISBN 0-694-00261-5 ISBN 0-690-04744-4 (lib. bdg.) ISBN 0-06-443280-7 (pbk.) 16 SCP 20 19 18 17 16 15 14

I want to be an astronaut,

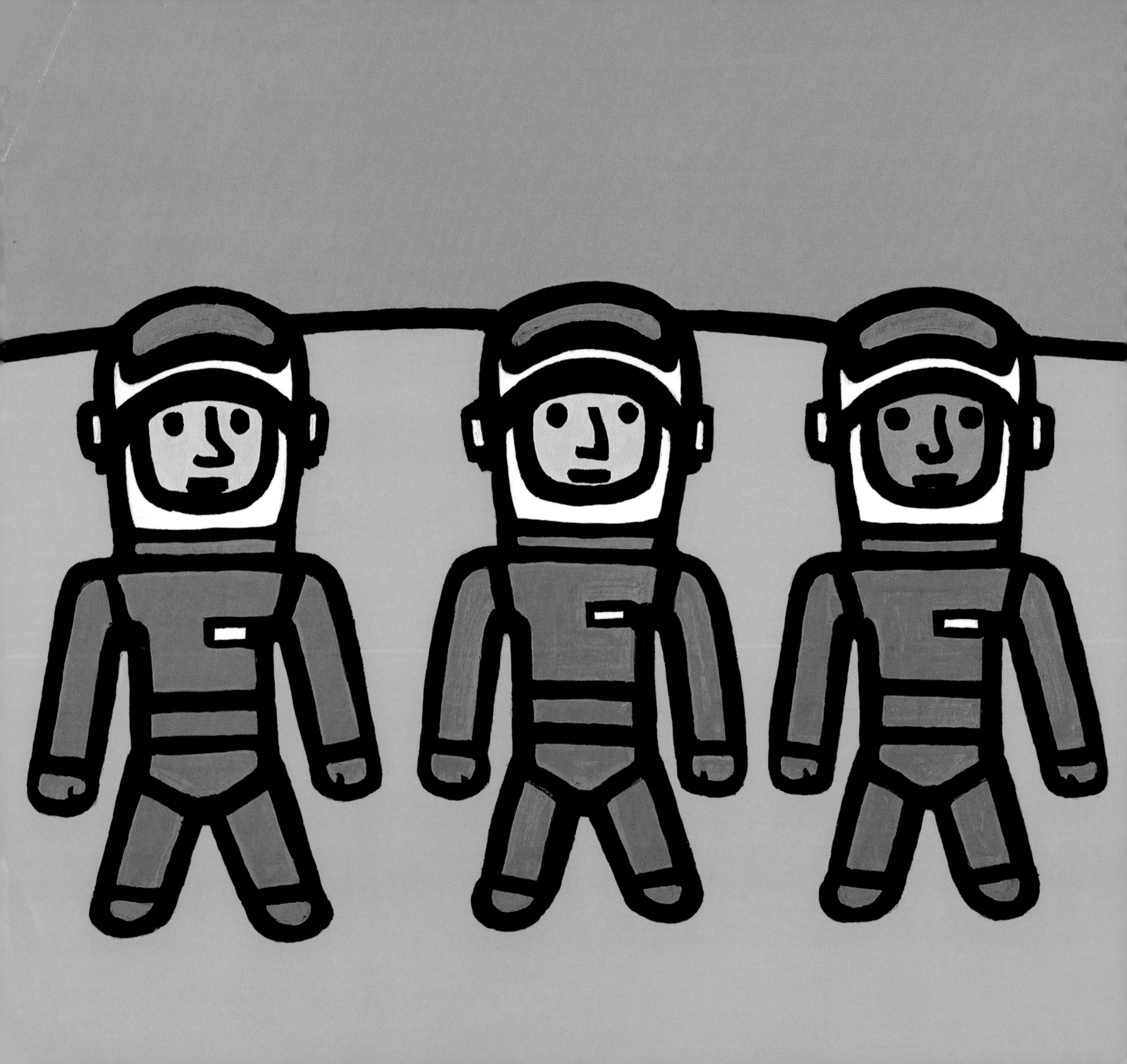

a member of the crew,

and fly on the shuttle

into outer space.

I want to be up there

on a space mission

and have ready-to-eat meals

and sleep in zero gravity.

I want to put on a space suit

and walk around in space

and help fix a satellite

and build a factory in orbit.

I want to be up there awhile

and then come back to Earth.

I just want to be an astronaut

and visit outer space.